Also by Michael Foreman:

Fortunately, Unfortunately

American edition published in 2013 by Andersen Press USA,

an imprint of Andersen Press Ltd.

www.andersenpressusa.com

First published in Great Britain in 2011 by Andersen Press Ltd.,

20 Vauxhall Bridge Road, London SW1V 2SA.

Published in Australia by Random House Australia Pty.,

Level 3, 100 Pacific Highway, North Sydney, NSW 2060.

Text and Illustration copyright © Michael Foreman, 2011

Distributed in the United States and Canada by

Lerner Publishing Group, Inc.

241 First Avenue North

Minneapolis, MN 55401 U.S.A.

www.lernerbooks.com

Color separated in Switzerland by Photolitho AG, Zürich.

Printed and bound in Malaysia by Tien Wah Press.

Michael Foreman has used watercolour and pastels in this book.

Library of Congress Cataloging-in-Publication Data Available.

ISBN: 978–1–4677–1213–2

1 – TWP – 8/3/12

This book has been printed on acid-free paper

Oh! If Only...

MICHAEL FOREMAN

ANDERSEN PRESS USA

Oh! If only . . .

I had stayed at home that day . . .

If only ... I hadn't met that dog ...

If only ... he didn't have that ball ...

If only . . . he didn't want to play . . .

If only . . . I was better at soccer
and hadn't tried to show off . . .

If only . . . the ball hadn't bounced down the hill . . .

And **if only** . . . the dog hadn't chased after it

and frightened the old lady's cats . . .

who frightened the birds . . .

who spooked the horses . . .

who wrecked . . .   the BIG PARADE . . .

and ruined the QUEEN'S BIRTHDAY!

And **if only** . . .
the dog hadn't continued
to chase the ball . . .

past all the sentries and the servants . . .

through the Palace and out again, wrecking the carpets . . .

and knocking over the birthday cake and lots of fancy stuff . . .

Oh! And if only...

he hadn't brought the ball back to *me* . . .

in front of all the world's TV cameras . . .

Oh! If only I had stayed home that day . . .

I wouldn't be the most embarrassed person in the

WHOLE WIDE WORLD!

BUT ...

If I had stayed at home that day . . .

I would never have met this great dog!